The HUNTERMAN and the CROCODILE

A WEST AFRICAN FOLKTALE

RETOLD AND ILLUSTRATED BY **Baba Wagué Diakité**

SCHOLASTIC PRESS / New York

Copyright©
1997 by Baba Wagué Diakité.
All rights reserved. Published by Scholastic Press,
a division of Scholastic Inc., *Publishers since 1920.*
No part of this publication may be reproduced, or stored in a
retrieval system, or transmitted in any form or by any means,
electronic, mechanical, photocopying, recording, or otherwise, without
written permission of the publisher. For information regarding permission,
write to Scholastic Inc., 555 Broadway, New York, NY 10012.
Library of Congress Cataloging-in-Publication Data
ISBN 0-590-89828-0
Diakité, Baba Wagué. The hunterman and the crocodile/retold and illustrated
by Baba Wagué Diakité.   p. cm.
Summary: Donso, a West African hunterman, learns the importance of living
in harmony with nature and the necessity of placing humans among, not
above, all other living things.   [1. Folklore—Africa, West.]   I. Title
PZ 8. 1. D 564 Cr   1997   398.2'0966'02—dc 20   [E]   95-25975
CIP AC
12 11 10 9 8 7 6 5 4 3 2 1   7 8 9/9 0 1 2/0
Printed in Singapore. First printing, March 1997
The illustrations in this book were painted on ceramic tile.
The display type was set in Pacific Clipper Bold.
The text type was set in 17 point
Neue Neuland Book. Book design
by Kristina Iulo.

To my mother,

Penda Diakité, who taught me that

hard work, honesty, and responsibility are

the tickets to existence in any society.

—B.W.D.

There was a time when Bamba the Crocodile took a pilgrimage to Mecca with his family. They traveled and traveled for many miles. But when their food and water diminished, and then finished, they became very tired and hungry and could barely walk. Luckily, they found some sweet shade of a baobab tree and settled down to rest.

Soon Donso the Hunterman was walking in the bush and was
surprised to discover the crocodile family.

"Bamba!" he said. "Why are you so far from the river?"

"Good intentions brought us here, but our food and legs gave
out," explained Bamba. "Can you return us to our home in the
water?"

"*Mook!*" said the hunterman. "You crocodiles are very well
known for biting people in the river. I will not take the chance."

With that, the crocodile wept and gnashed his teeth and

swore in the name of all creatures that he would not harm the

hunterman. And Donso finally agreed to carry them to the river.

"But how shall I do it?" Donso asked.

"Oh, that is simple," said Bamba, and he instructed the

hunterman how one carries four crocodiles on top of one's head.

Donso pulled some rope from his hunting bag and tied the

crocodiles' feet together. He stacked them, one on top of the

other, very neatly, then hoisted them onto his head.

Once at the riverside, Bamba the Crocodile begged Donso to carry them deeper into the river where the current ran strong. But when the hunterman did so, Bamba took Donso's hand between his great jaws and smiled. "You know, I haven't had anything to eat in a long time," he said. "Wouldn't I be foolish to let you go?"

The hunterman reminded Bamba of his promise, and they then argued at great length about right and wrong.

Soon an old cow came to the riverside to drink, and Donso begged her to help him. But the cow only said, *"Mook!* I will not interfere. Man does not respect others. Look at me. I spent my life providing milk and giving up my children to Man. Now that I am old, Man gives me no consideration. I don't care if Bamba eats you." Then the old cow turned and walked away — *dingi-donga, dingi-donga, dingi-donga* — with no guilt.

Next, an old horse came to the riverside, and the hunterman

pleaded for help. But the horse said, "Man is weak. I used to

help him plow his fields and haul big loads. But I was only beaten

for my helpfulness. *Mook!* I would be foolish to intervene. I

should let Bamba have you." After taking a long drink from the

river, the old horse turned and walked away — *ke-te-ba*,

ke-te-ba, *ke-te-ba* — with no guilt.

Next came a chicken, wondering what all the fuss was about, and Donso told her.

"*Mook, mook, mook!*" she said. "You do not deserve my help. Man takes my eggs — my children. And when he is very happy, he and his friends feast over my body. Bamba, eat him if you like." Ruffling her feathers and scratching up dust in the direction of the hunterman, she turned and walked away — *ko, ko, ko, ko* — with no guilt.

Next, an old mango tree that stood quietly by the riverside

spoke up. "Man does not deserve my sympathy," she said.

"Each season when I bear my sweet children, he takes them all.

When he is tired and hot, he enjoys my shade. But how does he

repay me? He cuts my limbs. And when I become too old to help

him, he will surely cut me down and burn me. *Mook!* Let Bamba

eat him," she said. And she waved her branches in the breeze —

sha, sha, sha — with no guilt.

At last, Rabbit, the most clever animal in the bush, passed by. When Donso begged for help and explained his predicament, Rabbit laughed out loud.

"How can someone put such a big and long load of crocodiles on his head? I don't believe it's possible."

"But it's true," Bamba insisted. And to prove it, Bamba and his family all came ashore with Donso the Hunterman and showed Rabbit just how it was done.

When Donso had tied the crocodiles securely to his head,

Rabbit said, "*Ho, ho, ho.* Here you are, Hunterman. Now you

can take your crocodiles home to your wife to make a great meal."

Donso was so grateful to the rabbit for his turn of fortune that

he invited him back to his village to join in the feast.

As they neared the village, they found that Donso's good

fortune had changed once again. A fellow villager greeted them

and regretfully informed Donso that his wife had fallen gravely ill.

The healer of the village had searched everywhere for the tears of

a crocodile to help cure the sick woman. But there were none to

be found.

When Donso heard this, he began to cry, for he loved his

wife dearly. Then he lifted the heavy load from his head and

addressed Bamba the Crocodile.

"Let these be the last tears any of us shed today, Bamba. I will

release you and your family in exchange for a few of your tears."

With this, the crocodile family shed tears of joy, which the

hunterman gathered quickly in his drinking gourd before rushing

home to save his wife.

Donso never forgot the lessons he learned from the cow, the

horse, the chicken, the mango tree, and the rabbit. From that

time forward he has reminded people of the importance of living

in harmony with nature and the necessity of placing Man among —

not above — all living things.

AUTHOR'S NOTE

*Awnithé .** Hello.

My name is Baba Wagué Diakité,† but most people call me Wagué. In Bambara, my language, Wagué means "Man of Trust." This name came from my grandfather. He was a great farmer and a caretaker of animals. He grew much food and fed the hungry. It pleases me to use his name.

I have long been known in my town, Bamako, for my drawing and storytelling. This is the way we teach children in my culture.

The greatest influences in my life have come from traditional stories told by my mother and my grandparents. As children, we loved to listen to their stories. They were our main source of entertainment. We looked forward to hearing them the way children today look forward to riding their bikes or seeing videos.

Our stories are much more than just entertainment. They give us encouragement and good morals. They educate us about our environment and the relationship between man and nature. They are basic to education in Africa.

I spent many years learning and dreaming about the animals, the trees, and the First Men from our stories. The First Men were good thinkers and hard workers. They respected the earth. I have been very curious about how their lives were in those first days. I wonder about

how it was in that span of time between them and us.

For thousands of years, their stories have been passed down to us orally. We must not forget the old ways of our ancestors and the lessons they taught us. And we must teach them to our children.

CLOSE COUSINS OF
THE HUNTERMAN AND THE CROCODILE

A version of this tale, called "The Ungrateful Serpent Returned to Captivity," is well known to folklorists. There are well over one hundred versions of this, widely distributed throughout the world, using various local animals as the freed animal. It appears as an Aesop's fable and as an Uncle Remus tale. Here are a few more versions to look for:

Han, Suzanne Crowder. *The Rabbit's Judgment.* Illustrated by Yumi Heo. New York: Henry Holt and Company, Inc., 1994. (Korean)

Ness, Caroline. "The Brahman, the Tiger, and the Six Judges." From *The Ocean of Story: Fairy Tales from India.* Illustrated by Jacqueline Mair. New York: Lothrop, Lee & Shephard Books, 1996. (Indian)

Torrence, Jackie. "Brer Possum's Dilemma." From *From Sea to Shining Sea: A Treasury of American Folklore and Folk Songs* by Amy L. Cohn. Illustrated by 15 Caldecott Medal and Honor Book artists. New York: Scholastic Inc., 1993. (African-American)

* OW - nee - chay   † ba - ba   wah - GAY   DJAH - kee - tay